ALLEGHGELLA

Cover design by Rafal Kucharczuk

Mask picture on the back cover presents the Shagodyoweh doorkeeper used in Seneca ritual. This was a pre-Civil War example by mask carver, Amos Snow. This is typical of doorkeeper carved masks used on Cattaraugus and Allegany Reservations of the Seneca Nation.

Editorial assistance from Kate Kelley

ISBNs: 979-8-9924689-0-8 (paperback), 979-8-9924689-1-5 (ebook)

1st edition 2025

[e5.30]

Dedicated to Rachel Matilda Place Newton (1895-1983).
She loved to write articles for the local papers about town events and community challenges, and private stories about woodland fairies and magical happenings that surrounded everyday life.

Contents

Foreword	VIII
Maps	XII
Wheel	1
Alleghgella	2
Fish on a Spear	4
Hums and Rattles	6
Stones at the Window	8
Mausolia's Lock	10
Indian Caves	12
Above the Tavern	14
Lady Luck's Last Card >	16
Two Rough Ashlars	20
Wolves Within	22
Scarlet Amanita >	24
Tail Chasing >	26
Kinnikinnick	28
The Hunt	30

Six Points and Alice de Trepagn 32

Eat Crow 36

Allie Myrtle's Rag > 38

Studebakers 40

Joined Askew 42

Keystone 44

Town Tea 46

My Perch 48

A Kami's Forest 50

Otter's Thorn 52

Buckeye Sweet 56

Triangles and Rectangles > 58

Oblong 62

Sharpest Knives in Town 64

A Mystery to Travel 66

Freedom Falls > 68

Say Uncle 70

River, My Reflection 72

Over Bridge 74

William Fox 76

Funky Chicken and Liberty 78

Hearth 82

Wildcatter Blues	84
Downstream Downstream	86
Minnie Springs	87
Spitting on Gnomes is Strictly Forbidden	88
Traveling Terrapin Trail	90
Rock Paper Scissors	92
Hidden in Leaves	94
Barrels on the Fiddle	96
Dancing with Hepatica	100
Baby Rattle	102
Final Cabin	104
Ruffled Feathers >	106
Chirp	108
Hogan's Floating Palace of Pleasure >	110
Annabella Rose >	112
Celestial Music Box	114
Three Thousand Arrows	117
Epilogue	118
Afterword	121

Foreword

River and the Medicine Bundle

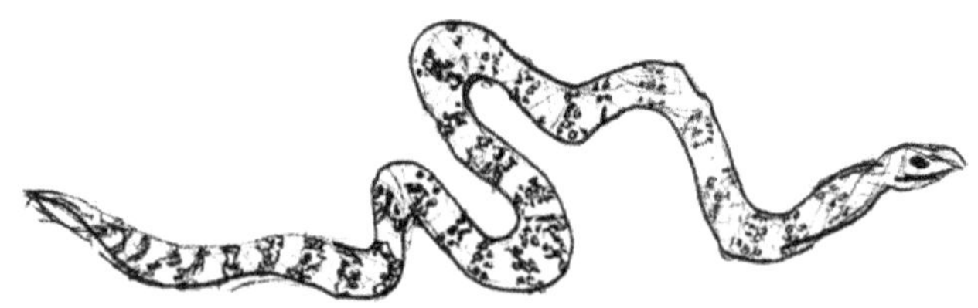

Rivers can snake.

One fall evening, I wandered off a wooded trail to follow the scent of birch smoke. I often walk these paths when returning to my childhood home in Emlenton, Pennsylvania, but I always welcome an excuse to detour. Smoke has a magnetic pull. Hopefully, it means someone is *now* by a fire. Following the scent of smoke, I crossed a gully that led me down into the Allegheny River valley to a campfire. As I approached, I recognized a familiar yet now older face of a long-lost best friend from childhood, River Vanderdown. We shared a complex, interwoven family history that is beyond what I can explain here. Our friendship ended decades ago, and much of our lives have passed without contact. He chose to live away from society while I pursued an urban lifestyle. Although he seemed to have remained close to the Allegheny Valley, our paths never crossed when I returned home. No one I have spoken to seems to remember him.

As a child, he spoke about seeing the future through time travel devices like arrows and feathers, and reciting incantations along the Allegheny River. He claimed to know secret entrances to time travel, which created fascinating adventures for us in the woods. His passion for time travel never wavered even after we outgrew playing in the woods. Into his late teens, he was consumed by his interest, but I had completely lost mine. This is why we had a falling out.

I hadn't expected to see him again and finding him in the woods that evening was a shock. He told me to stay by the fire while he retrieved something. As I waited, the flames receded and just embers glowed. After more than an hour, he returned with a wrapped collection of papers, which he called a *medicine bundle.*[1] He was soaked from wading in the river below, but the bundle was dry. It contained a stack of ragged, torn, and stained papers wrapped meticulously in green felt and leather. Some looked newer, while others appeared generations old. He had organized the papers with cards (mostly playing cards) attached to each piece, each oriented with an arrow. He said that the card order, associations, and orientations should be preserved. He emphasized, *"It was not only the contents but how life dealt it. "* And, sharing the medicine bundle with me, he said, was a saving grace for him.

He didn't stay for further conversation, so I learned little about his life through the decades after we lost touch, or how he collected the writings I am now sharing.

I cannot fully confirm the truth of all the stories. Some reference historical characters and events, while others involve people I have yet to learn about or stories that may or may not have actually occurred. Some are in the voices of the dead. Some of his writing reflects my own life experiences

---

1. A medicine bundle is a collection of sacred items in indigenous American cultures. The bundle is often used in ceremonies and represents a bridge to the beyond. They may reflect a collective identity for a group.

as he remembers them, but I promised to leave them untouched. The writing also seems to be seasoned at times with Grateful Dead lyrics.

Alleghgella is a bundle of stories, poems, and incantations that do not conform to a specific time period. Some pieces are myths and lore, while others are poems related to particular areas of the Allegheny River, and some may be considered incantations depending on the reader's experiences.

I heard the poet, Joy Harjo, say that a piece of writing can be a ceremony. If the piece connects with you, it will change you. And you can never be the same. So, beware when you read these pieces!

However River gathered or composed these writings, I hope they survive and a few pieces work their magic.

Travel safely, Brother River Vanderdown.

-Randolph Todd Newton

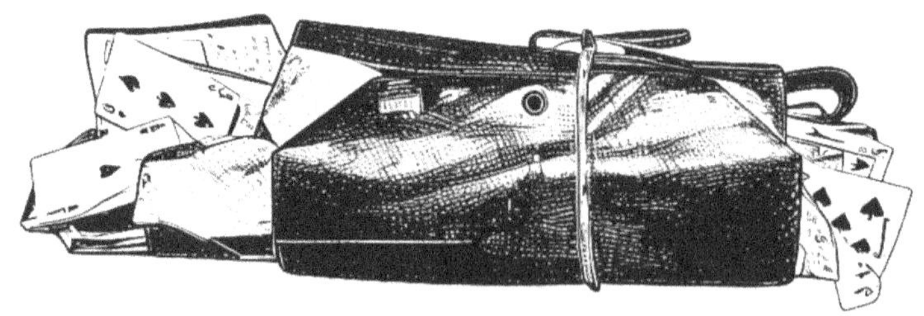

River's Medicine Bundle

Maps

The following maps show a portion of the Allegheny River and surroundings as reproduced from Edwin Babbitt's 1855 publication, *The Allegheny Pilot*. While this collection includes references beyond the portion of the river shown below, many of the stories are drawn from this stretch.

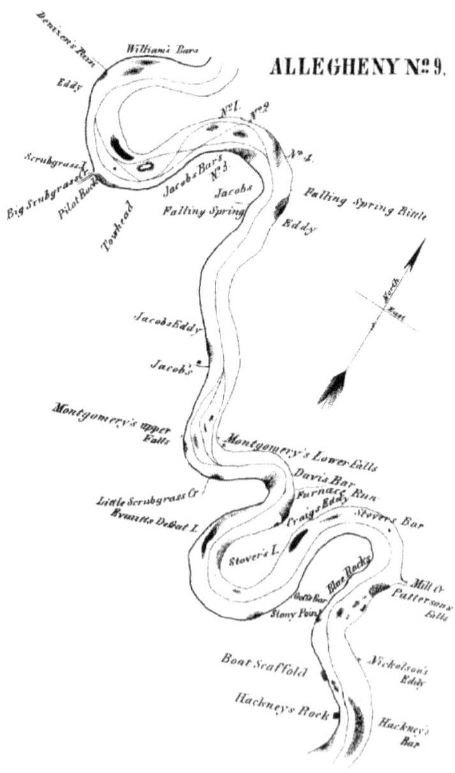

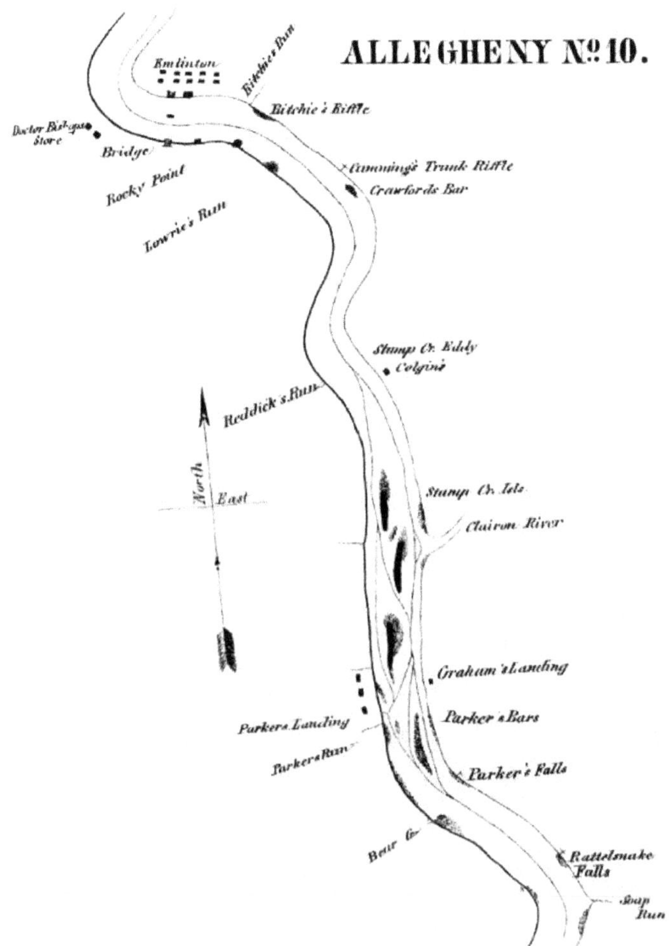
ALLEGHENY No 10.
Emlinton
Ritchie Run
Ritchie's Riffle
Doctor Bishops Store
Bridge
Cumming's Trunk Riffle
Rocky Point
Crawfords Bar
Lowrie's Run
Stump Cr. Eddy
Colgins
Reddick's Run
North
East
Stump Cr. Isls.
Clairon River
Graham's Landing
Parkers Landing
Parker's Bars
Parkers Run
Parker's Falls
Bear Cr.
Rattelsnake Falls
Soap Run
Wm Schuchman & Bro Lith. Pittsb.

Wheel

What is the alchemy that stirs
Between these parchment sheets?

It's the heart spilled into stories,
Dealt on life's felt table.

Cards flipping to show the mysteries:
Life's wheel paddling
On river waters, Loch Ness deep.

Alleghgella

An arrow in the air makes a tune, whistling
Music unique of Alleghgella.
The feather guides a person to dance through.

A bow stretched to pierce a clock's ticks.
Shot over the river and breaking time
With paper-thin planes of reality mixed.

Covered by webs in less-traveled corners,
Spun by celestial spiders,
The flint tip slides between life-path borders.

You reach a spot in a place almost the same
Although on the other side of the river,
The feather has created a temporal change.

Be cautious if you wish to travel this way.
You are taken to a different age.
Alas, you can peek, but you can not stay.

Paths left by aliens in patterns and colors,
Long kept encoded on wampums,
Shared discreetly in caverns and tavern cellars.

They said it was a tunnel underground.
A story told to distract the colonists
As a red herring when they came 'round.

Tribal shamans had their chuckles.
Secrets remained guarded
While pale faces were spelunking for tunnels.

To keep these paths known to humans,
Seneca entrusted John Reddick[1]
To guard the incantations and allusions.

The entrances and exits are hidden in pines
Off oddly marked trails,
Activated by arrow trajectories and rhymes.

You glimpse at another time when you cross.
Wishes and plans are often disrupted.
Resetting your life is part of the cost.

Wanting all possibilities but seeing what will be,
Like a bird in a cage with many feathers,
All flapping, wishing to be on arrows shooting free.

Thousands of directions, wanting free will,
Yet, only one life at a time,
On one paper, one feather picked for a quill.

---

1. **John Reddick** was an American soldier who fought along side George Washington at Valley Forge. He is buried in Parker, Pennsylvania.

Fish on a Spear

Fish on a Spear.
Not meant to be underwater here.
But Uncle Sam built a damn,
Flooding the top river valley land.

This story is not to be forgotten
Of Seneca land taken away.
The acres number ten thousand.
This history should be retold today.

Years passed of a treaty that lay intact
But the parchment ink eventually fades.
Those memories of handshakes past
Are now conveniently just reframed.

Pulled loose blanket cross-threads
Of Chiefs that signed with an X,
Unraveled oaths of blanket spreads
To speak for names that can not be read.

An agreement of dirt and space to stay unscathed,
The treaty was reserved as a vessel long ago.
Shattered and spilled promises contained,
A history over ages that fewer people know.

Now ripples to unnatural shores,
Echoes of cries for what is no more.
A lament for Fish on a Spear.[1]
Not meant to be underwater here.

---

1. Kinzua (Fish on a Spear): **Tgëdzó:a'** in Seneca , The flooding of ~10,000 acres in 1966 for the purpose of making the Kinzua Dam operational marked the breaking of the longest standing treaty, the Canandaigua Treaty of 1794 with the Seneca Nation. There was an alternative plan that offered routing water to Lake Erie that would not have broken the treaty.

Hums and Rattles

A night of adolescent restlessness growing up in a small rural town along the Allegheny River, within earshot of Interstate 80.

Those hums and rattles .... Bap-bap-bap!
Over the river, behind the treeline,

Brakes pop echoing over forest hills wild,
To me in bed, soothing my restless child.
The hum of the highway calms my struggles,
Yet, the mind takes sharp turns and I'm troubled.
Swerving, swerving, I'm still restless this night.

Spinning in the mind, my faulty AI,
Trying to slow down my mental sci-fi.
It is just me in the valley, kicking sand.
Hourglass filled to rally, and nothing planned:
Wayward car bots, spun out thoughts, life wisping by.

I stare through the window into space,
Swerving around my blocks, pumping the breaks.
Pull the window closed, and roll back to bed.
Trucks and cars still hum and rattle in my head.
What is this travel? Where is my home base?

All adventure lies ahead on that highway,
And I just keep skipping stones all day.
Wasting time tying useless mental knots,
Skips are wishes, just sinking thoughts.
What lies beyond the valley fog so gray?

My life! Like a day's dew on a semi's hood.
Wheeling through the Pennsylvania backwood
Just like one of ten thousand comets in space.
Give me a few lines shooting across the sky with grace.
Bones carry me through this ride and make good, not waste.

Stones at the Window

A habit of two young lovers as one stays at a friend's house and the other walks to work at the Quaker State Oil Refinery in 1922.

Our little game is routine.
I'll throw a stone to wake you
As I pass by at five fifteen
To hit Hill Street window as a cue.

Warmth to you as you rest in bed,
I walk past with an airborne plea,
Cautiously needling the thread,
As I dash to the refinery.

May my desire not break the pane,
Or be interpreted as spite,
Or that I might be insane,
But awaken you to happy daylight.

To risk the break of a window,
I would work a thousand hours of my time.
For a chance to hear a romantic secundo,
I'll pay it all till the final dime.

Let me avoid a bird's illusion
With just the tap of a rock.
That I may navigate from delusion
And not collide with an unseen thought.

A stone for acknowledging you
That I may catch a brief smile.
A tap from the love that I threw
Knowing I'll see you in a short while.

As each generation slowly passes
See the complexity of family toil,
Survival through all of our window cracks
And the final demise of the mortal coil.

I saw us through that dusty window;
You and my reflection, side by side.
Know through the pane to the end,
I loved you from outside to within.
The main vehicle was a simple tap
To welcome each other in.

Mausolia's Lock

Simple puzzles and mystery are described about a mausoleum.

Mausolia holds a challenge for the wandering soul.
Many see her structure as a cliff to another shore.
But for me, I'm only wanting a short puzzle to solve.
So begins a walk around her walls as I explore.

Mausolia is regal and patient,
As I feel around her green metal door.
Hidden within the portal's decorations
Lies a lock of red copper, shiny and pure.

Her pillars and stain-glass show beauty
With a puzzle to solve for a quick thrill.
But she enshrines a larger enigma
You won't solve with any mortal skill.

I am a child, just playing the game,
Fueled by adventure to find her lock.
Searching the crevices for a moving piece
That exposes a hidden, shiny copper part.

At her door, no one ever answers a knock.
I see the darker allure beyond her pane,
But to the other side, I don't plan to embark.
My search is for fun and to be entertained.

I jump for joy as I find her shiny copper lock.
A tactile riddle won to the ever-locked door!
She'll never entice me to stay long in this spot
Or convince me to lay on her marble floor.

I'll never need a key to the hidden lock
That opens to that place beyond our shore.
But, for today, I have a child's delight.
It's a puzzle played and nothing more.

Indian Caves

To walk
well past
the edge
of graves
down rocks
and brush
below,
small dog
in tow
to find
a cave
to where
the grass
won't grow.

Where myths
were born
that chiefs
did dwell
to sit
in dark
so calm
in peace
that swells.

To see
crawl down
in steep
descent.
Reflect
to tell
the time
of life
is brief.

Climb up. Ascend. Return. Lay down in grass by graves of past to rest a long sunbathe.

In hearts we know the tales to sow

To keep
our hopes
alive
for kin
to come
again
to have
the tale
retold.
To make
the myth
survive.

Above the Tavern

As the whistle blew across the river,
Friday night at the tavern went into full swing:
A crowd rushing from the refinery towards the liquor.
Workers cashing paychecks for weekend high jinks.

A boy snagged cards from a kitchen drawer,
Two streets down, another grabbed coins and bills
And chips collected from Grandpa's parlor floor.
Five boys gathered to hone their poker skills.

Assembled upstairs, above the tavern,
They learned their betting in the rough.
Like their ancestors in some woodsy cabin,
Playing hands, reading eyes, and calling bluffs.

Entranced by the game, the cards, and the stares,
The moans across the hall were not a care,
Nor the lively commotions of yells downstairs.
They focused on raises and calls, flushes and pairs.

No need for any hard drinks.
Money exchanged was just petty cash.
And none took passes of sugary winks.
Winnings taken home were only memorable laughs.

Lady Luck's Last Card >

A fateful steamboat trip to Pittsburgh along the Ohio River in 1870.

The steamboat was a-rollin'
A'travelin up the riverway.
Archie's hard-earned wages
Held close but soon stolen away.

After months of working in the quarry,
Cutting granite all day long,
Headed back home to Pittsburgh,
As he whistled an old Scot's song.

Cards were dealt with bourbons
And extra shine from pocket flasks.
Smiling West Virginia maidens
Offered winks and flirting laughs.

Lady Luck seemed so certain
As the players enjoyed more drinks.
Just card-playing distractions:
A solid recipe for a boat's high jinx.

Archie had a lucky feeling
As he watched his wages swell.
But the boat swiped another,
And sounded its evacuation bell.

The captain had found an island
Where he'd wait until the waters tamed.
Aground, passengers disembarked;
Here, Archie's luck quickly waned.

Ruffians were a'waitin
And he didn't have a prayer.
It really didn't matter
If all the card dealing had been fair.

Struck on the head, mauled and beaten,
The crowd passed by without a care.
All of his money was taken
On that dark river island lair.

Lady Luck dealt the last of the cards,
An Ace of Spades, to call his body home.
No more marks did this mason carve
On the face of any quarry stone.

A tragedy as common to relate
As the story of Cane and Abel.
This was Elder Archie's untimely fate,
Just like a stonemason's fable.

Epilogue

Not the story's true end.
   His son, also Archie, carried on the work,

Became an apprentice of his father's friend,
At Sandy Lake, as his father did in Perth.

He set up shop
Near an Allegheny River bank
There, he often whistled and pondered,
While chipping stones on a river plank -

What of society do we understand
And what of the water that stirs our boat?
The rocking may not be Nature's hand,
But just a reckless crew afloat.

Two Rough Ashlars

A young artisan, Archie Senior, sets up his stoneworks shop and makes the local newspaper in multiple ways around 1881.

Chipping away at a rough stone one night in the shop
Young and industrious, by the river was a beautiful spot
I was a new mason in town, ready to carve my mark
Excitement about the local lassies gave an extra spark

As I was closing, a beautiful lady peeked through the door
She threw a smile in my direction that I could not ignore
Our eyes got wide, and our conversation got thick
My chiseling tools were tossed aside, and our minds took a dip
(well, we had a nip)

As the candles burnt to the wick, we lost the score
Down the street, a few tavern revelers stumbled out the door
I caught someone spying through the curtain in my store
I suppose we gave them a nightcap to add to the town lore

Desires won and ruled in the night
We surrendered and let our angles fight
The morning sunlight brought a scurry
I, back to work - we both made a hurry

As I was enjoying the paper later that week, what did I see
Look! A wonderful article talking about me
Sharing that I delivered several fine monuments of stone
I was so proud of the appreciation the community had shown

But I also saw a mention that did not leave me alone
Alluding to something salacious, written in a cautious tone
To a young artisan to remember late-night shop discretion
The line was for me, but my name was not mentioned

Carrot and stick, I was the proud ass in between
Public eyes felt obliged to intervene
There was a thirst to wag judging fingers
In such a small place, these stories linger

My earthly toil is history now,
I lay under a marker on a brow.
Tools laid down, my work complete,
My shop has long vanished from River Street.

Subduing our actions is the work of life,
Chipping away to avoid all our suffering and strife.
And now, my body is but dust and bones.
Be careful to judge, for we are all rough stones.

Wolves Within

A wild wolf,
Crazy wolf.
What do I see?
Who are these creatures I am entwined with?
Who dwells so deep inside the forest of *me*?
Knocking towards a rocky cliff,
Rollin' down the hill,
Tumbling, I think we're three in a rift.
I blame them for my reckless spill!

A good wolf,
Or bad wolf?
Which will it be?
Which of these siblings should be nurtured?
And, what feeds this scuffle of *we*?
Untangled and growling so fervid,
My pain makes me angry.
I realize I am just one wolf, turned
Against the other wolf in me.

Bound to follow wherever I will dare,
I must concede both wolves are mine to bear.
We'll find our curvy way to home,
Tumbling and feeling every twist
That breaks my every bone,
For whatever lessons this may teach.
Until that final bellowing howl,
When the mountain perch is reached,
And the wolves resolve to cease our brawl.

Then I'll watch them break through, unbound,
Free and prancing into the holy forest ground.

Scarlet Amanita >

This seems to be a combination of tales about Mineral Springs and mysterious woodland beings as a parallel telling of Scarlet Begonias, but in a different realm. Ritchey Run is the stream that moves through Mineral Springs Park, and Charlie Horse is an old swimming hole there that has been popular for generations.

I was hiking 'round Mineral Springs,
Not for the cool air but a dip in the streams.
Behind the waterfall, partly secluded,
I spotted scarlet fungi in the moss.
It looked like a fairy as an illusion.
I stripped down and swam over to quell my thoughts.

Wading as water drops sparkled in the sun,
I watched them plop and dance on Ritchey Run.
But then I was pulled under and heard a laugh.
There was Amanita, and the tale had begun.
She still wore her veil and scarlet cap
Just like at Charlie Horse when I was young.

In the thick of the evening, when the rain got rough,
She stayed coy, and I hoped it wasn't a bluff.
As we sheltered, laughing under the fall's cliff,
I leaned for a kiss but quickly then slipped.
All that happens is carved on a rock as a glyph.
It's centuries old, but she keeps the same script.

My slip follows the way the legend unfolds.
She has done this for ages, but she never looks old.
You rarely encounter a woodland fairy,
Or kiss her like it goes in the song.
She shows up bringing sunshine, acting so cheery.
But it's very brief; she never stays long.

Well, there ain't nothing wrong with magic and ruse
Or Amanita, the forest's hidden muse.
There is nothing wrong with her scarlet cap
Or the way that she flaunts her waggin' tail.
I should have just enjoyed my time with her.
Sometimes, it's best not to pull away the veil.

Leaves of the valley whisper ballads serene
As the soil shines gold, and the water flows green.
Bells jangle from Amanita's anklets
As we all admire how the forest rings.
Hikers greeting hikers, joining in chorus,
Singing together by the heart of gold springs.

Tail Chasing >

Sweet scents fly through the air
A nod, we stress it's fair
The magic of a glance awaits
As bodies waving like snakes
Flames dance on faces circled around
As the fire crackles, discussions rattle
There is a closing of the ranks
Laughs and stories cease
As the scents of red maple escape
Pass the whiskey, for goodness' sake!
Listen to what you have heard
Has the scalping been deferred?

Blankets presented
Wampums exchanged
Smoke the peace pipe, play the game
With an X sign your name
Treaties and boundaries so human
Just fearful quandaries within

Created only in our minds
Invisible lines defined
Obligational binds
Society's illusions extended
We are fools - just pretended

What's yours what's mine
We fight and take - accept it as fine
This land was made for you and me
And we contort to make it *be*
Tokens exchanged over the hills
Yet no stopping the blood that sheds
The cup of trust is broken and spills
Down the creek beds
A sudden crick in many necks
We all see red
Twisting back to see fires spread
Lit by greed's chronic ruse
History is deja vu

Looking back, still no regret
You can see it's all true
We love each other
Fire and trees dancing together
A forest repeatedly flamed, ever so tribal
Caught in this deceptive cycle
Let the kiln fire another cup
Trust pours in again; new borders rise up
To quench our own thirst
While we smash our neighbors cup
All for the grace of Wind
Is destruction love's twin?
Just humanity chasing its own tail again.

Kinnikinnick

Kinnikinnick is a Native American herbal smoking mixture made from tree leaves, barks, and tobacco. It was used for ceremonies or partaken during fireside discussions.

Can what I think
Change what you think
I think you can change what I think
Kinnikinnick

Like a spell with repeated rehearsal
Let's share that smoke
And walk in a circle
With ideas as spokes
Connecting our centers in transversal
We each as dots
Spots understood if debated in reversal

Wheels rolling together
To move the great vehicle along
Stay within the lines in all talks we weather
And our material errors will never be long

The Hunt

Listening to an evening asylum of loons
With his little foxy brain all scattered,
He started a prance
And ended up battered.

This fox had hopes for a little theater
To show those vixens his croons.
But then he encountered wolves
And now is licking his wounds.

Crawling under the bushes,
He's wandered down to the creek.
Washing blood from his coat,
All his cleverness now in defeat.

Morning shines soon in the forest.
He sees a new imagined prey.
This is his playful chance
To shake off last night's foray.

It's just a butterfly, out of reach;
One he won't catch or even annoy.
But he is euphoric about the hunt;
It restores his life's hope and joy.

Six Points and Alice de Trepagn

Near Six Points, a wayward abode
In the sticks, near three crossed dirt roads,
There gathered an old-time jug band
Joined by three generations spanned.
Three by three sitting in a circle,
Nine passing elixirs during a rehearsal!

Passing around Wild Turkey bottles
To better preserve the older fossils.
Embracing that gold penicillin
While strumming tunes of old Bob Dylan.
I was just howling right along.
My friend, Kerly, stomping to the song.

We spotted headlights from up the way.
Who stumbled upon us or had gone astray?
A solo lass entered in a gush of cold wind.
A déjà vu seemed to pull me right in.
She seemed to travel from back in time,
And her gaze pulled me into her mind.

Barely on the rails, I saw trouble ahead.
I heard the whistle as she took my bend.
Around, around her red dress spun
Like an alert to an accident with illusion of fun.
Flashing her cards, I fell for this djinni that night.
I still held wishes as my heart felt her knife.

She spread the tarot and flipped the cup,
Read the leaves to see what fate struck.
Once surveyed, she went on to say,
"Ya gotta take the hand of Lady Luck to play.
That sixteen-spoked wheel keeps turning. Hold on.
Enjoy the spinning before your day is gone!"

She finally said her name, Alice de Trepagn.
With fortunes read, she led me along,
Swerving the wheel, steering the night,
Like an outlaw costumed in white.
I knew right away the road we were on,
Veered off a path, muddy and long.

Her sharp stare pulled me into dark waters.
I couldn't resist. I wanted to tumbled under.
Into her head, deep streams flowed,
Thoughts behind the falls I ached to know.
The whole evening was a bottomless pool,
But I was destine to simply play the fool.

In her wink, I felt a strong hex;
Dutch barn patterns as ideas, lines intersect.
She offered a charm for a kiss;
My mind's lines crossed the edge and I slipped.
That's when I surrendered into a tryst,
Swallowed into passion, waters and mist.

I emerged with a mindset changed.
Be it cold, I had rearranged.
Alice de picked up her cards.
She left to follow those merry bards.
Set off in the cold rain and snow,
On the road and another show.

Now mature and with time to replay,
I remember the words she said on that day.
I live in hand with chance and luck;
I embrace the wheel, even when it feels stuck.
If it spins around fast, I know to hold on.
The hex passed, but the charm has never gone.

I remain with passions subdued,
And peacefully broken-hearted.
Alas, I'm grateful that I enjoyed the spinning,
And the experience with Alice, I have never discarded.

Eat Crow

Eat crow.
Damn so.
How so?
I did
not so
good though.
I feel
far low,
too low.
Crawl in
the tomb
down low.
But still,
I will
show up
tomorrow.

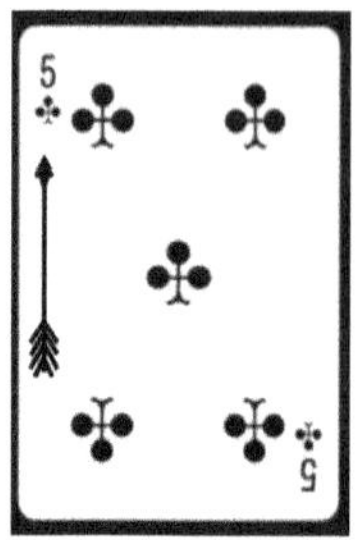

Allie Myrtle's Rag >

Social bonding I have always condoned.
Watching people parading town with their masks
As I sip fernet on my porch alone.
They each walk Main Street in their own charade,
But they whisper that *I* am the renegade.

Foxily trotting down a path in between,
Passing kitchen windows and church steeples,
Using the back steps avoids a scene.
Or two-step to the front door with an excuse,
Asking for sugar is my playful ruse.

Play the cards and enjoy the mingles,
Wading deeper into the waters,
Full houses and pairs, not just the singles.
For my ways, I have no plan to repent.
No apology to lovers' heirs for lives bent.

Swivel and hold sway, my rag is discrete.
Just pandering to people's desires.
I dance crazy but you won't hear my feet.
With cane and hat, they enter my den,
Leaving with one less bone and lesser men.

Kings and deuces may play a different score,
But they're all the wild ones that I'm dealt.
Both give me winning hands that I adore.
Smiling clowns each with a jester's frown,
Ashes to ashes, all the same in the ground.

The rumors my hand would hold in this town
Kept adding bones to my closet.
They're dividends for my thorny, worn crown.
No man dared cross me or my spouse
Else I'd turn you into a church mouse.

Spin my shadowy game as you so wish
With rumors that I'm casting dark spells.
But in truth, I was just a hot dish.
If ever I was crossed, I'd ferally burn,
Shade beyond ashes in a burial urn.

In spirit I now dwell where we have sung,
Under the same roof, now last rites are heard.
Instead of a waltz, now the dirge is done.
All kiss well in the funeral parlor and lament
A last chance to dance, the final dollar spent.

If you hear my whisper from the back street way,
Know it's me that's calling you hither.
I'm a ghost so it can't get too risqué.
I'll appear from the corner in the night.
I won't steal bones, but I'll flash a voluptuous sight.

Studebakers

Allie and her husband have a showy conflict.

You went ahead and bought a Studebaker.
Without me.
Rolling out of Bishop's dealership,
Flashing it around town
With so much glee.
Cause I was playing around
Even though you know I'm free.
Well, honey, that's fine. Now.
I bought a Studebaker for me.
It's gonna sit in the garage.
It'll take your shade,
But the shine's all for me.

Joined Askew

There's a little popup nestled up the river.
Tasty offerings in a tiny hotel.
It's a dicey establishment,
Built on slippery rocks where none should dwell.

To quench a thirst and feed a hunger
In ways always known to sell.
They don't openly advertise,
And it's best you don't even tell.

There's a peculiar wage,
It keeps both workers and clientele.
They are ever building a yearning
To return to that little popup hotel.

It's a crooked path to this place.
It's such a deadly itch for a crave,
To escape only to return,
Washed back to shore or sunken grave.

A wreckless swim into an eddy
That spins you down so quick.
Don't grasp onto rotting sweepers.
You can't be saved by a dead tree's stick.

But there can be a divine healing
To stop the mind from this tailspin.
The peace that surpasses understanding
Can repair the restless heart within.

I saw you at Sunday church.
We both know where we've been.
I see the money drop in the plate.
Like a boomerang, it hits back to me again.

To me, to my heart, to my chagrin
That bill that I spent the other night,
Now you softly offer in the plate.
Tricks aside, let's untangle our plight.

There's a path to straighten
What was first joined askew.
Take a break from all our snakin'
And make a fresh start, just me and you.

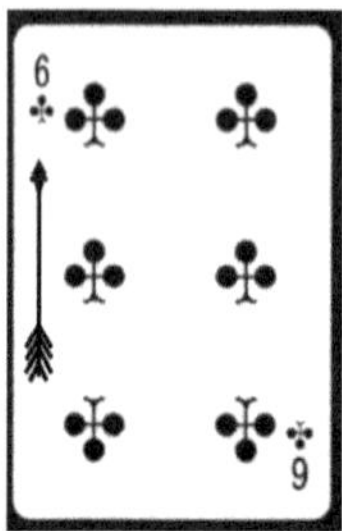

Keystone

Archie Senior takes a stone and tools from his shop down to the Allegheny River bank to work and reflect on his purpose in 1905.

If my hammer could break off the sharper parts
To smooth the roughness of injured hearts,
Or cement over cracked pieces of a life,
Or chisel kinder marks to lighten their strife.

If I could use my craft to extract their hurt
Or remove anger that remained in the air,
To square what was crooked to a right
Or heal friendships that ended in fights.

Where a life ends is where my labor starts,
Crafting a reminder of their earthly mark.
While they now dwell in some ethereal rank,
I remain toiling on this rocky river bank.

Sweating and cutting as boats paddle by,
I sometimes feel the deceased by my side.
Was there a corner in their time left unbeveled?
My tools can't fix what their lives left unsettled.

But on that same bank, I labor on my soul.
I struggle to chisel, shape, and find my role.
To be odd, not square, and rejected. Is it fair?
Are my slants a weakness or God's purposed error?

Two sides angled, I fill a gap to make my mark.
A wedge for opposing sides so they don't fall apart.
A keystone is how I fit; it's how I am carved,
To hold a living arch of people together is my charge.

Town Tea

Birds of ruffled feathers gather.
Pouring hot town tea,
Nestled together, I need to be there.
I don't want them talking about me!

What are we serving today?
Have they caught that sweet outlaw, Paralee?
Do you know who is rolling in the hay?
Has the hatchet been buried with Allie May?
Who plowed over the sign at the corner?
Who blew up at the town council dinner?
What were the winks in church between those two?
Oh, they're secretly together? Well, that's new.
Who got drunk and lost in the night?
And what parcel border prompted that recent bar fight?
Who's got a side-hustle with a few bedroom cams?
Has he been streaming for only fans?
How is the cornfield finally yielding?
And which of your wolves have *you* been feeding?

Sharing these mundane topics and the more risque,
Town tea stays warm until something hotter
Pours from rumors brewed for the following day.

My Perch

My childhood perch
Is where I'd often be;
Looking over the hills,
Writing notes and smoking tea.

Sitting on the edge,
A high rock in the valley.
With paper and pencil,
In a small ceremony,
Writing to me,
To my imagination,
Of what I want to be.

Folded into a plane,
I'd pray and send my wish free.

Now returning to that perch,
I still want to see
Through the clouds.
Where is this flight of me bound?

The perch has changed.
Growth taken hold again.

What I see
Is not what I knew.
Yet, it's new beauty.
And for the moment,
I appreciate that I am just to be.

A Kami's Forest

Kami are various playful and mischievous spirits of nature, possibly of ancestral origin. The term comes from the Japanese native religion, Shinto. *It is believed Kami are invisible and inhabit a parallel existence.*

Hear three chirps as a mystical call
By a snipe inviting you through a woodland hall.
This only happens on a Strawberry Moon
When the water flows over the petroglyphs
On Parker's Landing[1] that day, by noon.
These things by happenstance align.
The portal appears at half past nine.

---

1. In the Allegheny River watershed, Native American engravings called petroglyphs remain on rocks and are only visible during the summer dry months. Archaeological investigations have confirmed that the creators of these engravings were prehistoric inhabitants of the unglaciated Allegheny Plateau. The Parkers Landing Petroglyphs site along the Allegheny River in Clarion County is one of the rarest and perhaps the most significant.

Down thirty-three steps from Jacob's Ladder,
You are led through a place of vines and tatter
By little dancing Kami showing the way
To an arch opening and a mist of gray.
You enter a forest like an old Shinto story,
Between two oaks, there's a wooden torii.

Dirt rests atop a slow-moving terrapin
Where ferns grow as fractals again and again,
Splitting wild Fibonacci sequences
Rooted into so many crevices within.
Overhead shines bolts and steely fibers,
Webs that Kami weave like grannies on porch gliders.

Moisture catches between the threads,
By celestial cues, then plops into leafy beds,
As a metronome sounds the rhythm,
Music comes from a forest's hidden floorway
Like Kennerdell orchestras back in the day.

Trust the flashing thoughts cupped in your hands.
Kami grow them, even as ineffable plans.
Ideas as fireflies dance in your head.
It's the Grand Artist's canvas full spread.

A picture of a pure land we ache to see,
Between the heart and the hopes of what life can be.
Now paint with brush strokes guided by these magic folks.
Colors and love in the art that is shown before us,
Inspiration from the spirits shining in the Kami's Forest.

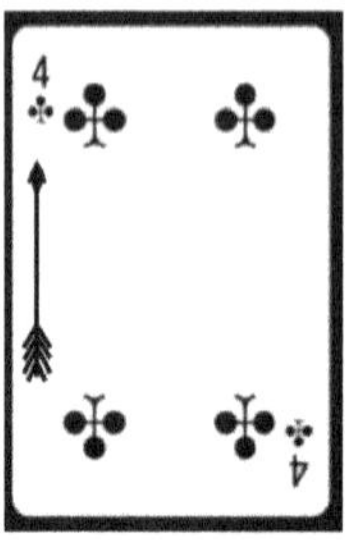

Otter's Thorn

Ask

Charades crafted and collected
   Take a lot of mental time.
   You can spend all day in loops.
   An exquisite mask you show
   Makes appearances fine.

   I will tell you a story.
   For me, it was true.
   But did it happen in *this* reality?
   That interpretation is for you.

   I heard of a Medicine Otter
   Who offered a thorn.
   A little pain to endure,
   A pluck from a Lion's crown
   To release loops that occur.

Seek

There exists the Dawando,
    A society of Seneca women.
    They talk with otters
    In the dark winter season.
    The otters offer thorns.
    They hurt but exist for a reason.

    Picked up on a snowy trail
    With a chattery noggin.
    It was like a mystical ambulance
    As a heady toboggan.

    Sledding to an opening of pines,
    All surrounding me
    Near a tumbledown shack
    In Venango County
    In a secret pact
    Assembled quietly.
    They led me to a place.

Knock

Tobacco was thrown.
    As I started to sit,
    I heard a knock from within.
    Then, I gathered my wit,
    And with that rhythm,
    Ceremony had begun.

Open

Rustling from the grass
   Appeared the Medicine Otter.
   Shook his coat and his ass
   But in a serious manner.

   He waddled atop a stump
   And started with a prayer.
   I suspected this was bunk,
   But I'd listen, to be fair.

See

The door was unlocked,
   And the otter guided me in.
   Poking and swimming
   Sliding into my mind's den.

   Shooting past tangles,
   And driftwood and straws.
   The thorn had suddenly pierced,
   I could now see my truth, my flaws.

   A hole to let in the full universe
   Flooded by alien applause.
   A soul in a meat suit is an exercise
   Accepting frailty yet finding cause.

Close

The otter gave a wink and a quiver.
  With only one plop,
  He swam off into the river.
  A piece of Lion's crown
  As a thorn delivered.

  I soon fell asleep.
  And when I awoke,
  Curled up on the ground,
  The fire was just smoke.
  The Otter Society was gone.

Reflection

A new sight to life was given
  The Medicine Otter had pierced
  And the loops left my bodies' system.
  With the pain of a thorn,
  Not society's chains,
  Nor a priest's collar.
  That's the surgical magic
  Of the wild Medicine Otter.

Buckeye Sweet

Jerry is a stone's throw away
With the band jamming full-score.
Chris smiles with straw hanging from his mouth,
Wiggling feet on the earthen floor.

The stage was framed in waving wheat
like a rural scene in a Van Gogh.
Despite the Beetle going south,
We still caught the start of the show.

We'd been thumbing on I-80
And hitched an Ohio ride.
Headed to Buckeye? Sweet! Jump in.
Oh the gifts that strangers provide.

Hey now, fast forward the concert tape
From Wall of Sound to Sphere sky light.[1]
After years on this Space mission,
The stage has evolved in-flight.

We lost friends along the journey,
And band players have changed.
Although the same music keeps playing,
Life is what has rearranged.

Do I see an eye of providence
Or just a piece of candy?
I still embrace a sugar-coated peace
And devour it with glee.

Like a buckeye sweet for the taking,
I pick one from the sheet.
A communion of sweet crushed nuts,
Some of them just like me.

It's all a brief skeleton pageant
In life's sparkle and flash.
We're all hitching a ride on a busy highway
To reach the music, to share a dance.

---

1. **Wall of Sound** refers to a large scale sound system designed explicitly for the Grateful Dead shows in 1973 by Owsley "Bear" Stanley. **Sphere** refers to the Las Vegas venue which hosts Dead and Company in residence starting in 2024.

Triangles and Rectangles >

This is the perennial story of one group claiming land where another had dwelled and developed culture over time: the cycle of claiming, surveying, dividing, taxing, oppressing and repeated assimilation. This poem is specific to western Pennsylvania, but aspects are relevant to a larger culture. The Dawes Act of 1887 attempted to force assimilation by breaking up tribal land into individual ownership and using the surplus for further assimilation programs. This included separating children from parents by sending them to trade schools, banning tribal songs, and removing native languages from daily life.

The awkward shapes that men craft,
Spread across a table, paper with Penn.
Triangles and rectangles with plots in draft,
Lands as future grants to immigrant men,
Frontiers as signed over by Dickinson.
Surveyors dream of reaching high pines,
Then watching them fall for cabin designs.

Cut into shapes as enticing tracts.
Nature untampered since the glacial thaw
Now a puzzle composed of polygon maps.
Divided by a settler's hand with a quill.
A drawing to move people against their will.
Obey the curving rivers, the carved ravines,
Hunting paths and pen-drawn lines unseen.

Shapes mapped and over time believed
Like an anthem, you better sing along.
With invisible threads over land so weaved
Stitched into green plots, we're attached.
Fed as providence; deceived.
Parceled land as morsels of freedom bites,
Polygons of private land. My rights!

Land carved for political bellies,
Private pieces to include us all
In a web of taxes and levies.
We all get chained to the ball with acres
As little paper squares, titles from Quakers.
Pulled into the illusion with whispers,
Fight for land against natives and winters.

The shapes spread as colonization expands,
Promises pale of Dawes private land dream.
The tribal way ceases; the tribal songs banned.
No place for a Longhouse in this grand scheme.
Become a little gear and crank into the machine.
"To kill the Indian and save the man," toss the sage!
Self-righteousness is all the rage.

When do shapes become too small to sow?
We stumble all over this rock.
Claiming every space to fight and grow.
Then, find another rock and turn it green
Like new celestial land to mow.
Some new yard, decorated vanity scene,
Critiqued by some future Thoreau.

Aliens must be amused at how we divide a place.
Maps of shapes, just now drawn in outerspace.

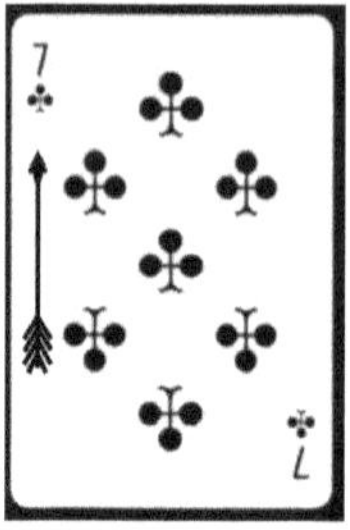

Oblong

I concede.
Show me an oblong bone.
A prize to hide and mark with a headstone.
Around it, a plot of dirt and grass to roam,
I'll dig around and enjoy it with care.
Make it a funky abode. It is fair,
To break my back and consider it home,
With a fire in a hearth to call my own.
A life of an ancestor imagined.
   Imagined like Leslie Sloan.[1]
Enjoy a garden and dig a hole,
Still looking for that buried oblong bone.

---

1. Leslie Sloan was a local farmer, carpenter, and oil producer in the mid-1800s along the
Allegheny River. He spent most of his life in the Emlenton and Scrubgrass areas.

I'd like to fall steep on the last stair
    To my attic -
    There's too much shit up there -
At the last rung of the ladder,
    As I reach for baby Jesus and Christmas decor,
    Not die in tubes, morphined and unaware.
Just moved to the cold porch with sun warming my hair,
    Put on a Space Odyssey score
    And possibly a little morphine if you can spare.
Then plopped into that long hole right over there.
I dug the whole thing. Part of me was that prize bone.
I'll finally fall in and give one last moan.
The certain return of dirt to that oblong home.

Sharpest Knives in Town

I lived with my wife in Tionesta
Til' I found her in bed with the milkman.
Turns out she was wide awake during her siesta,
So I traveled downriver in search of a new plan.

I decided to pick up a handy job,
Going door to door sharpening knives.
Plenty of women found delight
That I was willing to be paid in kind.

I lived in a shack, but that was okay.
I admit I barely made a dime,
But the craft has a particular precision
I worked hard to perfect over time.

Things get dull in many a' kitchen,
And that's when they'd call me around.
I made sure all the women were satisfied
With the sharpest knives in town.

Now I sharpen knives for a cutlery store.
It's more money, but I don't pick my clientele.
Sometimes, the knife sets come with more asks than I desire,
But I have always promised not to tell.

A Mystery to Travel

We turtles balance this earth
    as we watch humans consume.
Always hungry, expanding girth,
    Chasing a full monte or moon.

The tricks I play when coyote knocks,
    legs pull under my shell.
Three-card monte between the rocks,
    when dealt, where I am, he can't tell.

It's a riddle coyote never solves,
    yet he survives all the same.
Humans try solving hungers as puzzles,
    to quell innate desire is a meaningless game.

We all travel along river paths,
    Along glacier-carved ways.
Humans keep changing their use.
    A lot of toil for such a short stay.

Pondering in my river pools,
    humans crisscrossing my tracks.
They are very sophisticated fools,
    like coyote but wielding a bigger hack.

Ways carved by settler's axe.
    Then steam engine's roar,
Running down old river paths,
    ways vanished into distant lore.

Now, replacing old railroad tracks,
    are river bicycle trails.
Thirsty sapiens peddle right past
    in search of tasty ales.

No hiding from their traffic or phones,
    I'm a celebrity many a' day.
Take the selfie, but leave me alone.
    Quench that thirst to put nature on display.

Unanswered riddles surround,
    so heed Mother Nature's call.
It's turtles all the way down:
    Mysteries to travel that need never be solved.

Freedom Falls >

Freedom falls
Quickly down
Cold streaming
Ripples of media echo around
Cold Truth calls out and reaches
Her hand extending from the water below

No sponsors here
No ads for beer
Not televised
Just you and her, naked in the woods, no chains
Untethered from little devices
Not entwined with government reins

Ledge jump
Sudden shock
Shivering
Into an ice-cold ancient thought
Awakened just for a second
At Now's altar, again she calls out

Freedom falls
Raw and cold
Freedom glistens
Sometimes with fool's gold
Don't let Truth slip on peddled religion
Pull her up fast
Before she sinks in superstition.

Say Uncle

Saw you cookin' from a hibachi outside your van.
Heard you're hidin' out, traveling the sphere.
Hey now, I know you're disguised, Uncle Sam!
Heard you were drilling oil and skinning deer.
Now you're part of the circus, selling tabs stage rear.
Waiting for lines on cheap rides and fishin' dry creeks,
Working a Ferris wheel for politico freaks.

Your crowd has ladies of class.
Dealing with stacked decks, for sure.
They're harlots. Sorry, I didn't want to be brash.
They're picking your pockets as you roll on the floor.
Digging deep, I can tell what's in store.
Baking with your sugar, selling out the back,
Sweet tarts turned sour from all that smack.

Say Uncle, do you remember who I am?
I've grown while you've worked that crooked wheel.
See the country; spend a few days with me.
Leave Barnum at the bank with his rusted steel.
No arm twist but let him spin his greedy deal.
Let's kayak to The Point[1] for an ice-cold Straub.
Just listen to the music and follow Arrow.[2]
You can do better than that circus job.

---

1. *Three Rivers Point in Pittsburgh, Pennsylvania, and the name of Nilsson's musical movie,* The Point.

2. *Small dog in* The Point. *Also, an arrow shot invoking Alleghgella.*

River, My Reflection

River called to me one cool day   I called to you one hot day
                    My childhood friend
Let us play   I wanted you to play
                         By the river
                    Under the bridge way
He found a path   I found the path
To the place of fairies   I knew the place of fairies
He said he wanted to stay   I told you we should stay
                          But yet
I still stood far away   You fearfully ran away
Until I heard him yell   Until I let out a howl
Then I ran   I had been pulled down
Now to find   In a swirl caught
An older man   In life's troubles, drowned
                    Gasping in the river
                      In the current

I saw him   You saw me
Breath in prayer   God in air
I jumped in   You jumped free
Lifted his spirit   Pulled my spirit
                        From the eddy
I know River   You knew me better
A rebirth of me   I was revived
                      By grace of Wind
I saved him   I had survived
                    I saw my reflection
                      We did not die

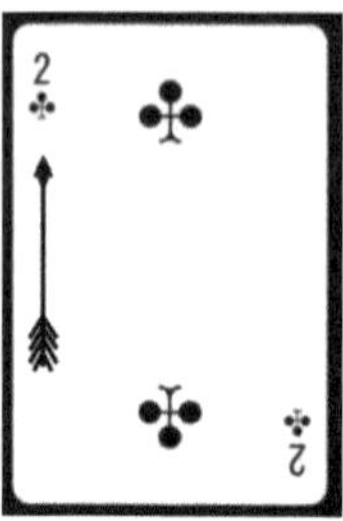

Over Bridge

Over Bridge, the ladies gather.
Civic building talks and cards,
With drinks of punch on the porch,
And leisurely things of that sort.

Big hats and flowery dresses,
Secrets shared of watercress patches,
Topics of country piety and protest,
And news of the local town *Progress.*[1]

Punch bowls filled with colorful sweetness
Floating, melting, party achievements.
Sherbet divided of reds and blues
Swirled and spiked with all the same booze.

---

1. *The Progress* is the name of the local town newspaper.

The bridge games they casually play,
Spinning to form what their men will say,
Pulling cards to see what will be the focus,
That's how they compose a crafty hypnosis.

Someone shouts a trump and takes a win.
That woman had her punch with three parts gin.
There's a bigger game at the next table:
These women are broader than parties, jeers, and labels.

"Eye eiddy" bridge is planned just downriver;
Some ladies are chatting with the bridge bidder.
Playing cards, steering roads, and picking acres,
Just small talks of civics at little card tables.

A town's progress is in building bridges,
Minds above the cards, punch bowls, and fishes.
Over chasms and labels, ideas formed as clay,
Fired into reality, the women are smarter in every way.

William Fox

This is the story of Mr. William Fox, president of the Foxburg and Clarion Railroad in 1880.

Clickety-click, wheels over rails,
Stitched together through low winding hills.
A steam engine choo-chooed twelve cars long.
Bolt links joined rails like the refrain in a song,
Made rhythm as wheels moved over gaps.
Mister William Fox with a box on his lap.

Soothing, picturesque, and rolling slow
To Clarion, with a gift to the court to bestow.
Serenades of steam, rails, and birdsong,
Pulling Fox to sleep as the wheels went along.
He hoped to present the boxed gun on arrival:
Evidence to support a criminal trial.

Conductor Cheitner was shot weeks before
By a peddler, Clancey, who broke the engine door.
The train was secured as the peddler fled.
Alas, Cheitner, the conductor, was dead.
Fox's trip to assist with the trial that day
Was sadly cut short on that same railway.

William Fox was sitting so silent and still.
He first carried the wrong box down the hill.
He had to run twice to catch one train:
Back home to fetch the right box and back again.
He ran for his life despite his heart's pain.
Then resting, his heartbeats began to wane.

The schedule was tight, all were aware.
Fox made the train, not a minute to spare.
Coal was added to make up for the delay.
The pullman observed Fox's head softly sway,
As the train rocked to the side and back.
It appeared William Fox was having a nap.

When the train pulled in, Fox did not care.
The pullman saw him still in his chair.
Fox's exit went unnoticed, devoid of a sound.
The reaper punched his ticket on the final outbound.
That was the fare paid for the evidence in the box:
The honorable fate of Mister William Fox.

Funky Chicken and Liberty

Riding out to Big Bend,[1]
Over the river, up the steep roadway,
Mom has her tennis game
So she takes me for a country stay.
Dropping me off at Peggy's place
As she does on those hot summer days.

Crackling gravel,
Turning off the road,
Up the long driveway,
I finally see the white trailer
Surrounded by marigolds.

There is Peggy with a cigarette
And in her pink morning robe.
AC is crankin' along,
No fans. It's country fancy
In this double-wide abode.

---

1. A location in the country, on top of the hills, overlooking the valley.

I'm breaking out the backdoor
And climbing up the trees.
Hanging from the branches,
Hypnotized by the fields
Ebbing and flowing with the breeze.

Finally, the lunch bell rings.
Running back to Peggy's place
She's servin' hot dogs and baked beans
With a big glass of sweet tea.
And I'm flying through our Grace.

Next starts the part I love the most.
Peggy puts the needle down with a grin:
Here comes the Funky Chicken.
Rufus' beats start with a punch.
I'm so excited to be dancing again!

Wiggling our knees and flapping our arms,
And singing my favorite dancing song.
This is the best an afternoon could be:
Prancing through all the trailer rooms,
Then out the door and on the lawn.

I hear the car coming up the driveway
There's no more Funky Chicken,
And no more drinking sweet tea.
I'll just have to wait til the next time,
When we'll do all this fun and dancing again.

It's a five-year-old's country paradise
To show the person that I'll grow to be:
I'm gonna dance to the Funky Chicken.
I'll wiggle and spin with all the fowl birds.
Oh, I'll make my life of liberty!

Hearth

Red hair
Red hair
Glistening flame
In the moon's light

Red hair
Red hair
Dancing around the fire
In burning delight

One for me
One for you
Only burning tips aglow
To close out the night

And now
The calm
Smoke floats as blooming flowers
Between us, only wishes flow

Sweet dreams
Sweet dreams
All smolderings left smoldering
Let me just huddle and stay.

Wildcatter Blues

An oil rush town, Antwerp City, was built up in the 1870s around a cluster of oil wells outside of what is now St. Petersburg, Pennsylvania. It was known to be a lively social and provisioning center for oil prospectors (referred to as wildcatters). Fatal accidents were common at this stage of the drilling industry. Nitroglycerine was used to "torpedo" the bottom of the well, increasing the oil flow (and profit). The explosion of nitroglycerine wagons was one type of fatal event that would periodically occur.

To Antwerp, I ventured with Eugene.
That's where I met my fiance, Nellie Cathleen,
Excited to make a fortune drilling oil.
That was the plan,
But Nellie took us down a road of betrayal.

We brothers split an acre purchase.
Soon, more than oil seeped to the surface.
We should have talked along the way,
But we stayed silent.
We were wildcatting night and day.

Eugene's pining for Nellie wasn't hidden.
He, too, was hopelessly smitten.
Her manner seemed so loving and true.
And we were brothers,
But we still fell for her deadly ruse.

One morning, I took the nitro wagon
Off to the well, but the wheel was dragging.
Then suddenly I hit a rock in the road.
That wagon took a dip,
The wheel fell off, and all of it did explode.

Eugene loosened the wheel the night before.
When it fell off, the nitro dropped to the floor.
It had the appearance of a mistake,
But I blew to smithereens
Because Eugene couldn't resist Nellie's bait.

Eugene was drinking later that night
From a bottle I mixed in fearful spite.
He prepared himself a cup of rock and rye
And took a strong sip.
With arsenic, I bade Eugene a belated goodbye.

This web of deceit was three-way spun.
She'd done no crime. We were the savage ones.
My scheme worked, but that was Nellie's plan.
We knocked each other off,
And that's how she pumped those wells and took our land.

From beyond the grave, I tell this story
For the hatchet with my brother to bury.
This wickedness could have been dispelled
If we weren't so focused on riches.
Our talks should have been at least as deep as that well.

Downstream Downstream

Downstream downstream
Let me float this one out
Let me travel through all my pain
   It's picturesque
   But my broken heart is spread about

Carried over rapids
I have no energy to care
I wish I were wilting rose petals
   That could drift away
   But instead my bones smash in despair

There is no salvaging
There is no easy cure
I'll trust the water and wind
   Carry me toward the next day
   Cupid don't you come around here anymore.

Minnie Springs

Minnie Springs, oh Minnie Springs,
There ain't no place I'd rather be.
Ice-cold streams with pouring rain
Crashing over the road, a fallen tree.

I'm back to slipping on her rocks.
Yet, it's where I want to be.
Now she's serving stormy weather,
Pebbles of hail pecking down upon me.

I've lost my balance in all her dirt.
Tumbling and falling to my knees.
Minnie pulled me under til it hurt.
Just a shot, no more iodine please!

Spitting on Gnomes is Strictly Forbidden

Lord Middy savors a new beechnut dip,
Squeezing his cheeks before his first swing.
As fresh tobacco moves across his lip,
He pauses until he hears the scramble bell ring.

The ball tees off with a miraculous flight
And rolls two feet from the pin.
Excited at the lay, he jumps in delight,
And does a cartwheel with a spin.

He didn't bother to look where he spit
Cause' that spit hit on the hat of a gnome.
And that gnome did take a helluva fit
As he wiped the spit off his tall red cone.

The gnome calls with a harrowing scream
And summons all the forest magic so hidden,
Turning the course into a chaotic scene.
Etiquette was broken:
Spitting on gnomes is strictly forbidden.

The squirrels emerged, shooting walnuts
From the trees at the fairway's edge.
Catapulting from little cannons
Aiming at poor Middy's head.

Sir Will's martini soon had a foul flavor,
But he was intent on sipping it again.
A beaver had added droppings to savor.
Will missed the ball and hurled his gin.

Sir Dick's clubs were dancing alive
As he chased them across the course.
The sticks had a Ceilidh on hole five.
Sir Dick was dancing, making matters worse.

Silver foxes in Sunday suites played fiddles
And danced around the greens,
Chanting short verses of pagan riddles,
Enticing lassies with medieval themes.

All waltzed until the sun withdrew,
And the frogs started ribbiting in chorus.
Like an old dark hillbilly hoodoo,
So known to be heard in these forests.

How could this little course be so cursed
Causing so many mulligans that day?
All the creatures were tricksters in concert
With St Andrew's spirit leading the way.

A caution to those who enjoy these nine holes.
Two instructions to avoid these magical tolls:
Don't partake in too many bowls.
And, above all, avoid spitting on the gnomes.

# Traveling Terrapin Trail

Leaves and twigs
    To rustle over and between
Passing sprigs
    My body is low and unseen

Rocks and mud
    To move over and around
Avoiding sludge
    I cover a little more ground

Grass and roots
    To squeeze past
Under droops
    I'm cautious not fast

Spruces and pines
    To dig under and through
Prickly sometimes
    Feet wriggle paddling a canoe

Fauna around
    To withdraw to my shell
Retreating not found
    My temporary farewell

Fungi and moss
    To squish and travel atop
Relaxing thoughts
    I break for a short stop

Wheels and feet
    This part is the most unknown
Oh, for St. Pete!
    Don't pick me up leave me alone

River and sand
    To feel water's edge
Moistening land
    Over pebbles to river ledge

Water and algae
    To wade into a pool for a cloak
Hiding in an alley
    Enjoy a backwater soak

Locomotives to bicycles
    Rails to trails nothing lasts
Gone over the hills
    Running down the old river paths

Terrapin trails
    Here long before biped maps
Cycles of human tales
    Brief crossings with turtle tracks

Rock Paper Scissors

Before the tossing of a rock to wake his love was routine, Archie Junior struggled with which route to take to the Quaker State Oil Refinery in 1922. One way went straight there, and the other went past the house where his love, the young lady visiting from out-of-town, was staying.

I have flown wishes on paper as rhyme.
I have launched arrows in hopes to cut through time.
Yet, what is left is to throw a rock,
And there is fear in this reckless thought.

Is this my desire for attention,
Or will I be served a muse's rejection?
I'll throw a stone to wake her up,
But while she is warm to me, I am freezing in doubt.

Is my path following an ancestor's torch,
Or will I be crying into bourbon on my own porch?
Will this end in a heart's impale,
Or bring to light what lies behind the window veil?

Don't forsake me til this theatre is done.
I'll break the fourth wall with a cast of one.
Two roads side-by-side exist:
One is safe, and the other a vulnerable twist.

One tosses a stone and risks a crack,
And the other straight to work and back.
Safely distant, it's a detour you might not travel,
Two roads intertwine in life with heart strings to unravel.

The way is never straight; each road has its bends.
There is no fan to fetch from the lion's den.
To be drawn into life with all its risky cracks,
Tripping because there are no scripts, no shown paths.

I'll hold my breath while my wish launches into the air.
Let it fly forth in bravery with a three-second prayer.
Be it a rock, sharp arrow tip, or folded paper plane,
Rochambeau[1] of love is a precarious game.

---

1. *Rochambeau* (aka Rock Paper Scissors) has multiple origin stories from many centuries ago. This particular name is attributed to Count Rochambeau, a French general who fought during the American Revolutionary War. Reputedly, he was a fan of the folk game.

Hidden in Leaves

Owls and foxes
Hidden in leaves
Spectrums of green
Origami folds
Flutter in the breeze
      The movements of all these creatures
         A cast of beings
            For a moment real

Hidden then leaves
Illusions in trees

Barrels on the Fiddle

One hot summer day in oil country,
My tale of deceit unfolds.
That I survived and she did not
I can't bear to be untold.

Paralee's train rolled into town.
Her face was glowing and fair,
With a smile stretching two miles long,
And gold in her curly bright hair.

She started fishing in the valley,
Joining right into the church choir.
While her voice was not angelic,
Attendance quickly shot much higher!

Single and young, she took a job
Tending at the town saloon.
She soon met a young oil worker,
A slender, dapper Johnny Moon.

Also, there was a Bobby Wollef
Who worked wells upriver.
And there was a Jeremiah Baer
Who labored near the miller.

In love, she had them all believe
That each had stolen her heart.
And in some romantic cahoots,
Each was feeling so smart.

Paralee was pulling the strings.
The men all played their parts.
Siphoning off oil barrels they loaded
To those in other carts.

Those barrels showed different labels
Written with Paralee's ink.
On barges to Pittsburgh to sell,
Deposited to her bank.

This was not the first fishing trip
For such a sweet outlaw.
Twas the third county for her angling.
She cast her lines without a single flaw.

One day she was caught with Bobby
In the woods by an oil well.
All the other men saw her
And that broke her heart string spell.

Oh, my beautiful Paralee,
Her safety was my wish.
I gave her a hasty farewell.
She gave me one last kiss.

Now I'm on the fiddle for June.
I know the deal, unlike before.
This oil heist is a two-way street.
Alas, Paralee plays this fiddle no more.

Dancing with Hepatica

Memories of a young boy with his mother in the cemetery and her mystical love of Hepatica.[1] *Some lines were identified as taken from his mother's story entitled "Adventures under a Rock" written in 1938 about a fairy Hepatica.*

A day visit to the cemetery
With the scents of Hepatica in the air,
Colorful wildflowers surround the wall,
Decorating graves is a frequent affair.

I'm hopping on one foot near the edge
On top of the old stone cemetery wall.
My eyes looked away from my mother's face,
"Keep skipping, Ranny, but try not to fall!"

---

1. Hepatica (Liverwort) is a plant associated with healing and protection, believed to ward off evil spirits. Hepatica symbolizes confidence and bravery, as it survives in harsh spring conditions. Native American tribes, including the Iroquois, valued Hepatica for its medicinal properties.

Emotions lifted by wildflowers,
She laughs and flashes me a long wide grin.
But she has a more profound sense
Of life's pains than I did back then.

Peering over the ledge at all the markers,
At each of those familiar weathered stones.
Ancestors' joys and tragedies now resting,
Mother reflects on sunny days and storms.

Echoing within us are their whispers.
Both good and bad still stir.
Mixed into our mind's processes,
Some act as personal saboteurs.

Hepatica kept Mother in balance,
And they'd dance along the cemetery wall.
It was always a lively chase to find flowers
Raising her spirit like a sunny morning bell.

You can't always mend life's broken fences.
Some stakes are rotted too deep to unearth.
You can't reverse others' past offenses
Or bitterness if they never felt self-worth.

But for an afternoon, Hepatica gives a hand,
And she'll dance over stones with you.
In her silent beauty, she will understand.
She helps you roll away the dew.

So, lay on the grass in the beauty she gives.
Join in a sunbath near stones of past kin,
Until you travel with the scents of her flowers,
When the four winds blow you home again.

Baby Rattle

Baby is soothed by her babbling shaker.
This turtle-shell rattle lulls her to sleep,
Peace within, to spread and keep.
The gift was crafted upriver, and down it flowed.
Passed to this baby, long ago voices on her bestowed.

Soothsayers imbued toothshakers to share
Calmness of ages, free of the Reaper's scare.
Teeth of beloved ancestors chatter within
Echoing like songs of faithful seraphim.
Oh, that they would tell their tales again.

Rattle rattle,
Let this sweet dream begin
And let this same shaker
Sooth her future kin.

Final Cabin

When I can't harvest honey,
    When I can't feed the fire,
    When I can't pick tomatoes,
    When I have lost my desire,
Just let the whole buzz be.
I am sorry. I am just thinking of me.

Don't let them max me out.
    Don't stretch out my longevity.
Kids, this is a matter of fact,
    Let this be a sacred pact.
Please cash me out.
    Let me go with dignity.

Don't wallow in the mire,
    Just leave me to the ravens.
Don't make it seem so dire,
    Make a party on the occasion.
Let the chips just fall,
    That's the best plan of all.

Go ahead and dance around my funeral pyre.
        You know I love a good smoke and fire.

Sorry, this has to be about me.
But here's how I want my end, I plea!
    Away from Big Pharma,
    I'd rather not bend that knee.
    Let me just enjoy my dharma,
    On this, can we agree?
Shell games of maxing out Medicaid
For the bills old folks never see,
Passed to the next generation's taxes paid.
I don't want that racket for you or for me.

Just leave me in a backwood cabin
    With some good provisions,
    With some goofy art that I've fashioned.
A place hidden in the trees
    With a fishing rod and a veggie garden.
Maybe add some weed plants,
        And Mycelicia,
        And a bottle of bourbon.
I'll thumb my nose
    And hang the family tartan.
Surrounded by nature,
That's what I want for my departing!

Ruffled Feathers >

My feathers get ruffled in the town store.
I get a scowl as I enter the church door.
When I walk off the street and into the bar,
They turn their heads
And start warming the tar.

A disruptive squawk from the other tree,
A disharmony spread from a bird off-key.
Those annoying fowls rub me the wrong way.
I don't like any of them,
Picking at me as their prey.

I already wear a plumage of troubles,
And those birds make my feathers ruffle.
Tripping me up, making me stumble.
I wish I had a little relief.
Today, they're due for a scuffle.

I retreat to the woods,
And hear all different chirps.
Then I see the cardinals,
I love to watch them flirt.
They live in peace without a care.
All the disorder in Nature still has harmony,
But what's the source of my ruffles that need repair?
Underneath the feathers, see the marks
From the teeth of my mind's own snare.

Chirp

Bird chirps in chorus,
Cut and fitted
Into waves.
Small sharp pieces
Dropping through leaves.
A song in stained glass,
Tangled notes and shooting rays.

Passing as dew drops
Landing in your ears.
Light chirps ricochet
Their dance calms your fears.

Colored through prisms
Glistening in your head.
From grace, peace ripples
Meandering crick bed.

Nature slows your mind.
Kindles your heart.
Sheds your weight.
Pass it on to the Divine.

Arise and follow
This sacrament as a cue.
Troubles forsaken,
Fly with a lighter heart, a path anew.

Hogan's Floating Palace of Pleasure >

In the 1870s, a Ben Hogan was banned from operating ill reputed establish-ments at Parker's Landing like his "gymnasium" which boasted of its focus on intense healthy physical exertion with a staff of mostly female coaches. So, he created a new establishment that stayed off land and could float to different counties beyond local authorities. This story is told by a card dealer employed on Ben Hogan's boat.

Teamed up with notorious French Kate
And adding the class of Kitty O'Brien,
All the county rules Ben Hogan skated
Were claimed by out-foxing and never by lying.

His pride was the Floating Palace of Pleasure.
That traveled the Allegheny waters.
Siphoning wealthy oilmen of their money
For all the joys they dare not tell their mothers.

They would wait along the river's edge
To be taken to the floating bordello
In cushioned chairs by a fine boat
That delivered many a well-heeled fellow.

There were games and business-minded women,
Both were unlawfully entwined.
But for the antics, towns could never blame him.
Floating on the waters eluded a sheriff's fines.

The women signaled with a flirt, not a word.
I dealt the crooked games as Hogan's pawn.
Taking cues to butter this rich man's bread,
That's how we hustled all night long.

Annabella Rose >

From the pen of a card dealer, this story describes his star-crossed love for Annabella Rose, one of the working women on Ben Hogan's Floating Palace of Pleasure.

While I'm dealing the table,
You're giving me flirting signs.
It's part of our nightly hustle.
You signal me the cards on time.

Oh, Annabella Rose, I can decipher
Extra gestures you throw to me.
I was dealt a flush of hearts for you,
And I'd bet all my wages happily.

I watch how you carry yourself.
I see all the tricks that you do.
I've seen how you play the game,
Stirring up all the men how you do.

I don't care how many you've hustled,
And I don't care where you've been.
I could skip a wish across this river for you
To reach the other shore against the wind.

When I see you come off the gangway,
And you walk out into the morning dew,
I hope that even in our silence,
You know all the love that I have for you.

I hope you take another look at me
When that boat comes to the shore.
We could say farewell to the Floating Palace
And lead this jagged life no more.

This Palace gig is a no-win scheme.
It's a leaky vessel that's drying you up.
I see the wilting of your stem.
Annabella, your petals are gonna' drop.

Alas, I'll see you tonight on the boat,
And we'll hustle and trick again.
I wish we'd just dive off the bow;
Away from this racket, we could swim.

Celestial Music Box

Years passed after the card dealer and Annabella moved on from the Floating Palace. Now much older, the card dealer includes this poem with one of his correspondences to Annabella in 1904.

Each landing on opposite sides of the river,
We're two arrows crafted from the same tree.
We're not separated forever,
But shot in diverging trajectories.

The shafts have now weathered and rotted,
Feathers torn and floated away.
The flint tips are buried and forgotten.
As fate, shared origins have decayed.

I have traveled on Alleghgella,
I saw our future as I flew across.
On return, I felt like a fortune teller.
So, I live with two parallel thoughts.

Between what I wished was a future,
And, Annabella, what I saw would be.
My heart broke when you left for California.
You were destined for a life far from me.

Knowing the songs before they play has a cost,
Reflections in waves from a future time
Flowing from a celestial music box,
But what plays out is still worth the same dime.

Life offers many sublime melodies
We share in this space-time machine.
We dance in different realities
With shared music over a vast ravine.

There's one more piece I saw in the future:
Two old folks on a bench as friends
Sharing intimate laughs and riddles.
That's what I look forward to until then.

I'll wait to hear that paddle wheel rhythm
As the river sings its sweet songs.
While that Floating Palace broke us down,
It is the river that will still carry us home.

Three Thousand Arrows

Three thousand arrows in different worlds launch.
    Which one is destined?
All trajectories hit my existence at once.
    Into one action,
Life's thoughts squeeze into one moment's bunch:
    Ichenin sanzen.[1]
All ink falls from my stories into a puddle.
    The world in my reflection.
A quill pokes me into a cold water plunge.

---

1. *Ichenin sanzen* is a Buddhist concept that translates to "three thousand realms in a single moment of life." It is a key concept of Nichiren Buddhism.

Epilogue

I conclude the *Alleghgella* collection with a Henry Wadsworth Longfellow poem that River included in his bundle.

The Builders

All are architects of Fate,
Working in these walls of Time;
Some with massive deeds and great,
Some with ornaments of rhyme.

Nothing useless is, or low;
Each thing in its place is best;
And what seems but idle show
Strengthens and supports the rest.

For the structure that we raise,
Time is with materials filled;
Our to-days and yesterdays
Are the blocks with which we build.

Truly shape and fashion these;
Leave no yawning gaps between;
Think not, because no man sees,
Such things will remain unseen.

In the elder days of Art,
Builders wrought with greatest care
Each minute and unseen part;
For the Gods see everywhere.

Let us do our work as well,
Both the unseen and the seen;
Make the house, where Gods may dwell,
Beautiful, entire, and clean.

Else our lives are incomplete,
Standing in these walls of Time,
Broken stairways, where the feet
Stumble as they seek to climb.

Build to-day, then, strong and sure,
With a firm and ample base;
And ascending and secure
Shall to-morrow find its place.

Thus alone can we attain
To those turrets, where the eye
Sees the world as one vast plain,
And one boundless reach of sky.

Afterword

As I collected and compiled River's papers into this book, I wanted to provide more context for some of the names that do relate to real people, but I did not want it to distract readers from the pieces themselves.

While a number of the writings contain referenced individuals assumed fictitious until I can fine some historical record, I am sharing short information about the names I am familiar with.

-R. Todd Newton

Persons

John Dickinson (1732-1808) was a founding father of the United States, known as the Penman of the Revolution for his writing "Letters from a Farmer in Pennsylvania." He often served as a second ghost writer for Thomas Jefferson. During his tenure as President of Pennsylvania (1782-1785), he signed many early settler land deeds in the Western Pennsylvania region.

Henry Dawes (1816-1903) was an attorney, a U.S. Senator, and State representative from Massachusetts. He is notable for the Dawes Act, which attempted to assimilate Native Americans by forced disassembly of tribal traditions and tribal ownerships.

William Penn (1644-1718) was an influential Quaker who founded the Province of Pennsylvania during early British colonization. Much of Penn's efforts in his lifetime served as a draft for ideas and expansion that would unfold after his death.

John Reddick (1740-1822) was a historical Revolutionary War patriot who had a long-standing friendship with George Washington. The first documented service was with Washington at the attack of Fort Duquesne in 1754 and he also served with Washington at Valley Forge. He settled along the Allegheny River area between what is now Emlenton and Foxburg, and is buried in Parker, Pennsylvania.

Leslie Sloan (1823-1897) was an early settler in the Allegheny area. Originally a carpenter and farmer, he also became a successful oil producer.

William Fox (1851-1880) was a member of the wealthy Fox family that settled in the area in the early 1800s, with various family members being successful enterpreneurs in oil and railroad. William Fox was a successful businessman prior to his untimely heart attack on a train, delivering evidence to a trial.

Chris Kerlin (1969-1991) (referred to as *Kerly* in Six Points and Alice de Trepagn and *Chris* in Buckeye Sweet) was born in Nickleville, Pennsylvania, lived near areas described by many of the stories. He was an adventurer, athlete, enjoyer of the Grateful Dead, and friend of many. He died at age 21 in a car accident outside Emlenton.

Archie Newton, *the Elder* (1828-1870), immigrated from Scotland to Kent, Ohio, then moved his family to Pittsburgh. He continued his trade as a stonecutter, often commuting down to quarries in the West Virginia area. His last, fateful trip home occurred on a steamboat from Morgantown to Pittsburgh along the Ohio River in 1870.

Archie Newton, *Senior* (1858-1937), son of Archie the Elder, was fatherless from the age of 12. His father's friend took Archie Senior under wing and steered him into a stonecutter apprenticeship at Sandy Lake, Pennsylvania. In 1881, he set up a shop in Emlenton, Pennsylvania on River Street, along the Allegheny River. He would often move a stone-cutting project down to the river bank and happily challenge anyone to a race swimming across the river. He was a life-long resident of the town and took great value in serving the community. At different points he served as burgess (mayor) of the town.

The following picture and article was identified to be associated with Archie Newton Senior :

EMLENTON EXANTHEM.

Festival-Personal-Drunk-At Frank-lin-Too Fresh-Two Capitalists.

From our Special Reporter.

EMLENTON, June 18.

E. Strong came down from Bradford on business Thursday.

Forrest Halings arrived from Oil City Friday and is spending a couple of days with his brother.

H. C. Bradley, a one time resident here, and very popular business man, now of Warren, Ohio, was in town Monday.

Porterfield & McCombs continue to receive and supply large numbers of customers at their large general store. It is good goods and reasonable prices that bring them.

E. L. Fleming is recovering slowly from his severe illness.

A. R. Newton, the marble cutter, set up several fine monuments this week. "Jerry" Caleb started for Warren to-day, where he expects to move his family soon.

Williams has one of the finest tonsorial parlors in this section, and yet he continues his improvements.

A strawberry and ice cream festival was held in Bennett's opera house last night for the benefit of the Presbyterian church. It was well attended and will be repeated to-night.

There is a young artisan in town—we will not say just who—that is hereby advised to be a little more discreet about taking company to his shop after business hours. The scandal is getting abroad.

Why does not Emlenton air itself each Fourth? There is plenty of capital here, and it is a good point. A little money invested in getting up some attractions for visitors would be some money... coffers from whence it came, and then it could not be said that her sister towns, St. Petersburg and Edenburg, had more enterprise.

Young Archie Senior (A.R. Newton in paper) and an Emlen-ton News article, both form 1881.

The article seems to give credence to the story told in the piece "Two Rough Ashlars."

Archie Newton, *Junior* (1893-1976), the son of Archie Senior, was a lifelong resident of Emlenton, Pennsylvania, working at the Quaker State Refinery his entire life, with only a break during WWI to serve in France. He was enamored by an out-of-town lady, Rachel Place, that would visit Emlenton to stay with her best friend from college. After a long courtship they were married and stayed in the community.

Arch Newton III (1929-2020), referred to as "Ranny" in "Dancing with Hepatica", the son of Archie Junior, was born in Emlenton and lived in Detroit and Pittsburgh. Eventually he resettled in Emlenton to have a family.

Kate LaCount (aka French Kate) (~1842-unknown), was a famed redheaded mistress of the oil region. She was known for running brothels and saloons in the western Pennsylvania regions of Pithole, Tidioute, and Parker's Landing. She had the name "French Kate" not because she was French, but because "French" implied anything goes. Kate would later partner up with Ben Hogan for business successes along the Allegheny River near Parker's Landing.

Kitty O'Brien (aka Kitty Bowers) (~1840-unknown). In a later phase of Ben Hogan's businesses, he partnered with Kitty. They parted ways when he gave her money to venture to Ohio to gather women and a bartender for a new saloon and brothel. She fell in love with a bartender she interviewed and used the funds for their honeymoon.

Benjamin Hogan (1840-1916) lived a life of well-documented adventures, chronicled in a biography he funded himself, among other books. His career started with thievery at age 14. He was a prize fighter, Midwest strongman, saloon and brothel owner, and gymnasium owner - often blending these roles. He typically began in a new area as a bouncer and card dealer. In later years, he imparted his card skills to trusted dealers he hired at his establishments. In the final stage of his life, he became a preacher and married a mission worker. He operated a flop house in Chicago and was more known as a humanitarian in that region.